With love to my godchild Sarah
and her brother Ian

First published in the United States 1993 by Dial Books
A Division of Penguin Books USA Inc.
375 Hudson Street, New York, New York 10014

Published in Great Britain 1993 by HarperCollins Publishers
as *Cats Among the Toys* · Copyright © 1993 by Lesley Anne Ivory
All rights reserved · Printed in Italy
First Edition
1 3 5 7 9 10 8 6 4 2

Library of Congress Cataloging in Publication Data
Ivory, Lesley Anne.
The birthday cat / Lesley Anne Ivory.—1st ed.
p.   cm.
Summary: On his birthday, a cat's favorite toy is hidden
by a mischievous rabbit, and finding it again takes him to many
other cats and toys.
ISBN 0-8037-1622-2
[1. Cats—Fiction.   2. Toys—Fiction.]   I. Title.
PZ7.I952B1   1993   [E]—dc20   93-129   CIP   AC

THE BIRTHDAY CAT

LESLEY ANNE IVORY

Dial Books *New York*

It was Octopussy's birthday. He loved all his presents, but his favorite was a little stuffed tiger. Octopussy decided to hide it in a safe place.

While the other cats were playing, Octopussy hid his tiger in the Noah's Ark. "Look after my tiger," he told the toy lion.

"Come play with us," called the rabbit family. The rabbits were fun. They were mischievous too, sometimes. Octopussy played tag with them for awhile. He didn't see one little rabbit hopping off with his tiger!

When he got tired of playing with the rabbits, Octopussy looked for something else to do. He saw the kittens playing marbles on the tile floor.

He saw a big cat named Gemma lying on the
Snakes and Ladders game board. She would
probably tell him to wash his paws or take a nap.
He decided not to disturb her.

Maybe I'll ride on the rocking cat, he thought. But his brother Manuel got there first and wouldn't get off.

Octopussy looked at the toy woodpecker on the wire. But he remembered that birds don't like to play with cats. Tigers do, though. I'll go and get my tiger, he thought.

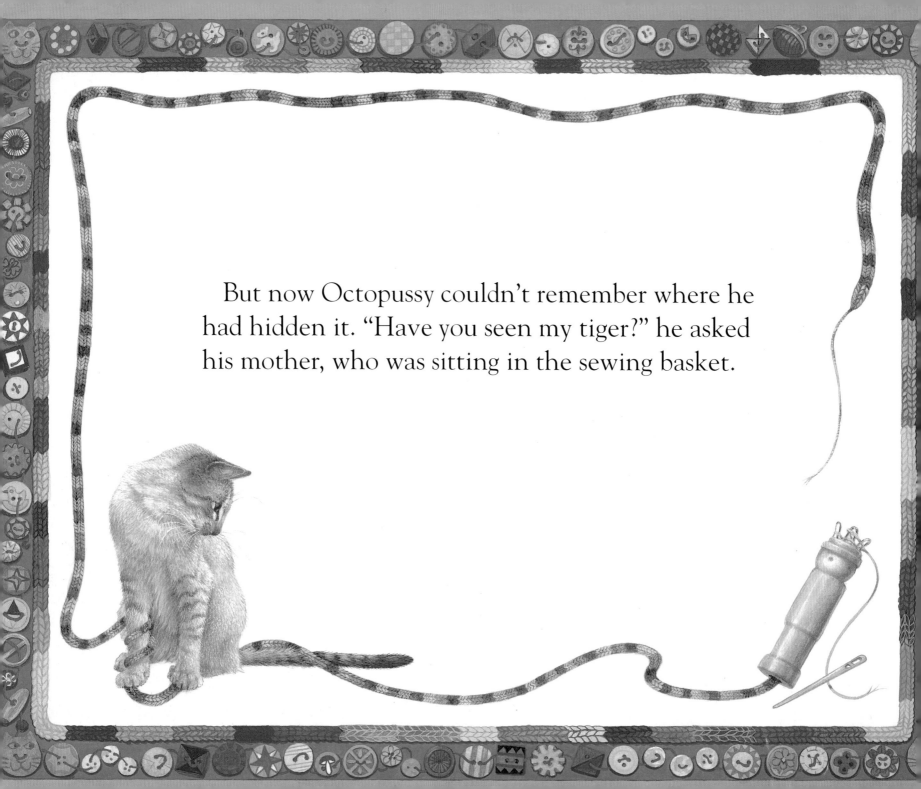

But now Octopussy couldn't remember where he had hidden it. "Have you seen my tiger?" he asked his mother, who was sitting in the sewing basket.

"No," she purred. She told him to wash his face
and then see if the tiger was visiting the dolls.
He looked in the dolls' basket. But it wasn't there.

"Have you seen my tiger?" he asked two kittens who were playing with blocks in front of the fireplace. But they were too busy to answer him. Octopussy began to feel very sad.

He thought he would hide inside the dollhouse until he felt better. *What was that in the dolls' bed, though?* It was his tiger!

How did it get there? Octopussy took the little tiger in his mouth, the way his mother used to carry him when he was a baby. He gave it a small nip for good measure. This time he would remember where it was, and he wouldn't tell anyone else!

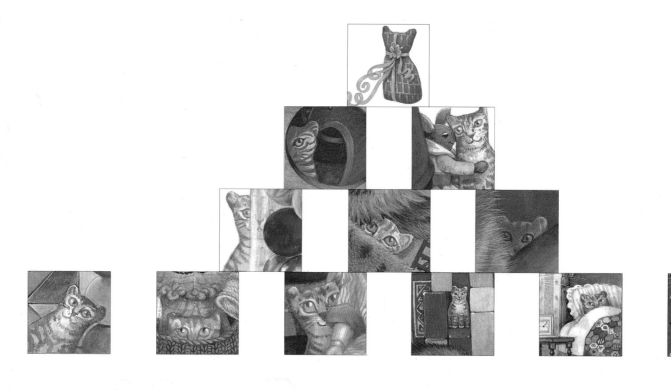